The Fairies of Starshine Meadow

Belle and the
Magic Makeover

Collect all the sparkling adventures of
The Fairies of Starshine Meadow!

The Fairies of Starshine Meadow

Belle and the Magic Makeover

Kate Bloom and Emma Pack

stripes

Fairy Lore

In Starshine Meadow, a grassy dell,
Shimmering fairies flutter and dwell.
Throughout the seasons they nurture and nourish,
Helping the plants and flowers to flourish.

To grant humans' wishes is the fairies' delight,
Spreading magic and happiness in day- and moonlight.
But to human beings, they must remain unseen,
So says their ruler, the Dandelion Queen.

When a wish has been made the fairies must speed,
Back to the meadow to start their good deed.
There they must seek the queen's permission,
Before setting off on their wish-granting mission.

And when the queen has agreed, wait they must,
For a sprinkling of her special wish-dust.
Then off they fly to help those who call,
Spreading their magic to one and all.

When a wish is made and fairies are near,
You can be certain that they will hear.
They'll work their magic to make a dream come true,
And leave a special fairy charm just for you!

For fairies love the secret work they do,
And a fairy promise is always true.
So next time you're lonely or full of woe,
Call on the fairies of Starshine Meadow!

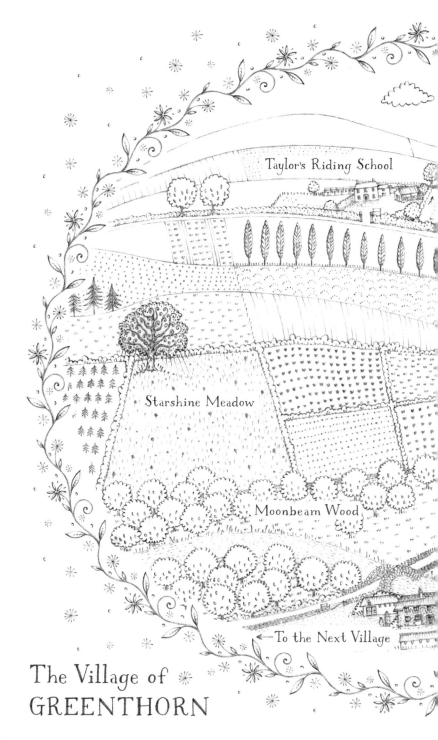

Taylor's Riding School

Starshine Meadow

Moonbeam Wood

← To the Next Village

The Village of
GREENTHORN

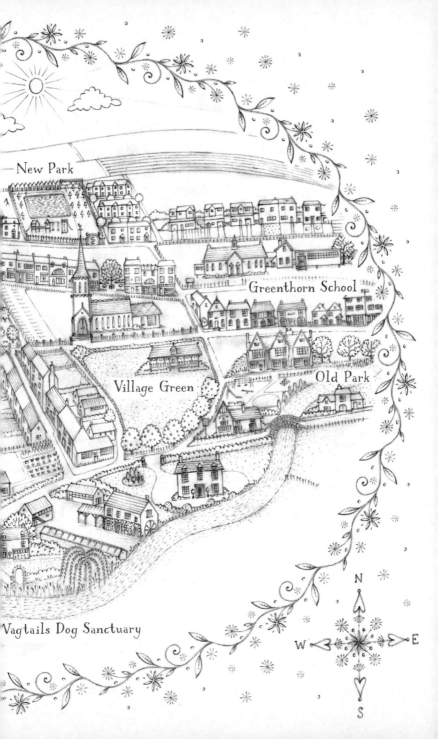

New Park

Greenthorn School

Village Green

Old Park

Vagtails Dog Sanctuary

N
W · E
S

To Olive Catherine, dearly loved and missed.
K B

With love to Mx, Gx and big D too!
E P

STRIPES PUBLISHING
An imprint of Magi Publications
1 The Coda Centre, 189 Munster Road, London SW6 6AW

A paperback original
First published in Great Britain in 2006

Characters created by Emma Pack
Text copyright © Susan Bentley, 2006
Illustrations copyright © Emma Pack, 2006
With thanks to Gail Yerrill

ISBN-10: 1-84715-001-2
ISBN-13: 978-1-84715-001-1

A CIP catalogue record for this book is available
from the British Library.

Printed and bound in Belgium by Proost

2 4 6 8 10 9 7 5 3 1

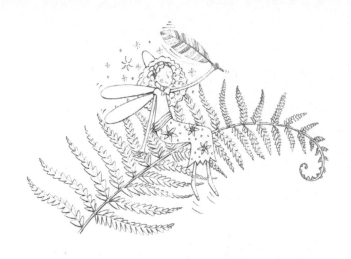

Chapter One

Bluebell sat on a fern leaf, fanning herself with a tiny feather. Her sparkly pale-blue wings drooped in the heat. She longed for rain, but the air was hot and still, just as it had been for the last few weeks.

Bluebell watched as a drowsy bumblebee flew down the overgrown track that led to Greenthorn.

Suddenly there was a flash of glittering yellow wings as a fairy darted past the bee and sped over the fence into the meadow.

"There you are, Belle!" cried a sunny voice.

"Daisy!" Bluebell grinned at her friend. "How can you fly so fast in this heat?"

"It's an emergency!" said Daisy, hovering in front of Bluebell. "The Dandelion Queen wants to talk to everyone. Come on!" She wore a dress of pink-tipped daisy petals, and her long blonde hair was tied in bunches.

"What's happened?" asked Bluebell. She fluttered up into the cloudless sky with Daisy, her springy dark hair fanning out around her.

"I don't know. But we'll soon find out!"

Bluebell and Daisy held hands as they flew up to join the shining stream of fairies that was pouring across Starshine Meadow towards the great oak.

The oak was home to the Dandelion Queen who ruled over the fairies. It stood in the corner of the meadow, just outside Greenthorn village.

"Belle! Daisy! Wait for us!" chorused two voices. With a flash of mixed pink and green light, two fairies zoomed up from the grass.

"Rose and Ivy!" Belle said delightedly. "Where have you been?"

"We've been sitting under some ivy leaves. It was lovely and cool," said Rose. "I had a wonderful daydream about paddling in a birdbath!"

Rose had pale brown hair down to her waist. She wore a dress of rose petals and her wings were a soft pink.

She linked hands with Bluebell.

"That sounds delightful!" said Bluebell, with a smile. "I can't remember it ever being so hot."

"Come on," said Daisy. "We'd better hurry."

Ivy flew over and linked hands with Daisy. She had sparkly pale-green wings and long red plaits and her green dress was made of ivy leaves. "Why do you think the Dandelion Queen has summoned us?" she asked.

"I'm not sure," said Daisy. "It's probably got something to do with this weather."

"I'm sure you're right," said Belle. "It's been really hard to keep our meadow flowers from wilting."

As they drew near the oak, Belle noticed a faint smell of dry bark, and all around the oak's trunk lay hundreds of crispy brown leaves.

Usually, at this time of year, every leaf on the oak glowed with magical fairy light, which to human beings looked just like sunlight shining through the branches. But today the leaves were glowing very faintly indeed.

"The oak doesn't look at all well," said Rose, frowning.

"It's lost lots of leaves," said Belle
worriedly, floating down and
landing on a branch. Rose, Ivy and
Daisy settled beside her.

A sound of tinkling bells came from a tiny arch in the trunk as the Dandelion Queen appeared, wearing a golden petal gown. Her silver blonde hair streamed down her back in spiral curls and her crown was a curling dandelion bud.

There was a hushed silence as the fairies waited for their queen to speak.

"Fairies, I have called you here for an important reason," the queen said. "I know how hard all of you have worked tending the meadow's flowers and grasses in this hot summer. But despite our help, the heat is causing our oak to lose many leaves. So I have decided to make it a special tonic, to give it the strength to grow new ones. I have a list of ingredients for each group of fairies to find. They must be collected by the crescent moon, in seven days' time."

"How exciting!" cried Daisy. "I wonder what will be on our list."

All the fairies looked eager to help, and they went to collect the lists, which were written on tiny fragments of bark.

When it was their turn, Bluebell came forward. The Dandelion Queen handed her the list for herself, Ivy, Daisy and Rose and then she smiled. "I shall need an especially beautiful bowl for the tonic too. Will you make it, please, Belle?"

"Of course, Your Majesty!" Bluebell replied delightedly. She loved making things and was always collecting pretty petals, starry mosses, and even shiny sweet wrappers that humans had thrown away. If any fairies needed a present, or a pretty party dress, they often asked Bluebell to make it.

When all the lists had been handed out, the queen wished the fairies good luck, and they flew off in all directions, eager to make a start.

Belle flew into the meadow and hovered over a patch of beautiful bright red poppies.

Ivy, Rose and Daisy crowded round to look at the list.

"An ivy leaf with eight points," Ivy read. "I'll find that."

"A petal from a red rose, growing on a bush with no thorns," Rose said. "I'll look for that."

"I can't see the list!" cried Daisy, fluttering up and down. She craned her neck to peer over Bluebell's shoulder.

"That's better. One petal from a daisy with exactly a hundred petals," she read. "I'll find that in two shakes of a lamb's tail!"

Bluebell, Ivy and Rose chuckled. Despite the heat, Daisy had more energy than a whole swarm of fireflies! Belle read the final entry on the list. "Oh, a white bluebell flower."

"Gosh, Belle, where are you going to find that?" asked Daisy.

Bluebell shook her head. White bluebells were very rare and usually only flowered in the spring. "I'm not sure," she said. "But maybe you can all help me look?"

"Of course we will!" chorused Ivy, Rose and Daisy.

Bluebell flew up high into the air. "Come on, I've thought of somewhere with lots of unusual flowers. Remember how we flew over to the park in Greenthorn when the flowerbeds were being planted in spring?"

With a whirring of fairy wings, Ivy, Daisy and Rose flew after her. "Wait for us!"

Chapter Two

Bluebell fluttered over the park gates and landed in a flowering bush. Her three friends flew down beside her. They looked around in dismay.

"Oh, dear," said Bluebell, gazing at the scorched grass and dry flowerbeds. "It wasn't like this a few months ago. It looks like no one's been here in ages."

Rose's face clouded. "Those poor flowers really need a drink."

"And there's litter everywhere!" Daisy flew over to a paper cup, which had blown under the bush. She peered into the cup, just as a sudden breeze flipped it on end and trapped her inside. "Help!" she called in a muffled voice. "Let me out!"

"I suppose we'd better rescue her!" Rose said to Ivy and Belle, trying not to laugh.

They flew down and tilted the cup on its side. Daisy zoomed straight out and shook out her crumpled skirts. "Yuck, what a horrible place to be trapped."

Bluebell smiled at her. "You're safe now. Let's start looking for our ingredients!"

Just as they were all flying up from the grass, someone came into the park.

"Quick!" Belle said urgently. "Hide!" She shot behind a leafy branch with Daisy. Rose and Ivy quickly joined them.

It was an important fairy law that fairies must never be seen by humans. The Dandelion Queen was very unhappy with any fairy who broke this rule, even if it was by accident. She had to make some special magic dust to sprinkle on the human, so they forgot everything they had seen.

The fairies watched as a man and two girls walked down the path.

"Here we are," said the man. "The perfect spot for enjoying the sunshine." He was tall with dark hair and was wearing shorts and a T-shirt.

The two girls didn't look so sure.

"Can't we go to the new park, Dad? It's got a paddling pool. This one's all dirty," said the older girl, tucking her black shoulder-length hair behind her ears. She looked about eight and had a pretty, heart-shaped face and big brown eyes.

The younger girl nodded. "I don't want to play here!" Her short curly hair framed a round face. She had big brown eyes too.

"Sorry, you two, but the new park's too far away," their dad replied. "Besides, I love it here. It's where I used to play when I was your age, and I like to think of the two newest members of the Lake family playing here too. But it's sad to see it looking so neglected."

"We know," said the older girl with a sigh, but she was laughing too. "You say that every time we come here! Right, Katy! Race you to the playground!"

"You're on!" Katy shouted, dashing after her. "Hey, Fiona! Wait for me!"

Their dad jogged after them.

"They look fun. Let's follow them," said Rose.

Taking care not to be seen, Bluebell, Ivy, Daisy and Rose flew over to the playground and hid behind a bench. There was an old mosaic on a nearby wall. It had tiles missing and part of it had been splashed with paint.

A lady in a flowery dress was walking her dog close by. She stopped as Fiona, Katy and Mr Lake appeared. "Hello, Dave. Hot isn't it?" she said. "Poor Muppet's feeling very warm in his fur coat!"

"Hi, Val! I bet he is, poor thing!"
said Mr Lake. He patted the top of
Muppet's head.

The scruffy little mongrel dog
gave a friendly yap.

"Hi, Mrs Roberts. Hi, Muppet,"
said Fiona. She and Katy bent down
to stroke Muppet.

"I bet he's delighted to see you two," Val said with a smile. "He's a bit bored today as I daren't let him off his lead in case he cuts himself on all the broken glass."

"It's sad to see the park looking so tired, isn't it? I suppose all the money has been spent on the new park," Dave said to Val. "The mosaic's looking the worse for wear too. It doesn't seem all that long ago that our class made it."

"Isn't it sad?" Ivy said, looking upset that the park was so unloved. Belle, Daisy and Rose nodded.

Fiona smiled up at her dad. "But Dad, it must be years since you and Val's son helped make the mosaic."

Val laughed. "You're right, Fiona!

I reckon it must be twenty years. This park was lovely when your dad and Andrew were little. It was always full of people having picnics and children playing." Her face softened and a dreamy expression came into her eyes. "I used to read fairy stories to my children under the trees. Do you know, Andrew once thought he glimpsed a fairy in the twilight?"

Bluebell, Ivy, Rose and Daisy exchanged delighted glances.

"A real fairy?" Fiona and Katy chorused, wide-eyed.

Their dad chuckled. "Yes, but no one believed him. Especially because he was a boy, and all boys know that fairies don't really exist!"

"Don't exist!" Daisy spluttered, starting to flutter up from her hiding place. "Of course we exist!"

Bluebell, Ivy and Rose only just managed to pull her back in time. "Calm down, Daisy!" Bluebell whispered.

"I've written to the council to see if they'll give the park a bit of a makeover," Val told Dave. "But I've heard rumours that it's being turned into a car park. I know there's a new park, but Muppet and I love this place and we're not the only ones."

Dave and Val came over and sat on the bench, and the fairies clustered together behind one of its legs, trying to keep out of view. Muppet spotted them and wagged his tail. Ivy put her finger to her lips. "Shh!" she whispered. "Good dog!"

Muppet lay down with his nose resting on his front paws and closed his eyes.

Fiona looked at Katy. "Do you think Mrs Roberts could be right? Do you think there really might be fairies in the park?"

Katy's eyes shone. "I don't know. Let's go on a fairy hunt!" She danced off across the grass to a flowerbed near a cherry tree and Fiona skipped after her.

Bluebell, Rose, Ivy and Daisy flew into the air and hid in the cherry tree.

They peered down as both girls began checking blossoms on a tall purple bellflower.

"No sign of any fairies," said Fiona.

"That's because we're up here!" Rose whispered gleefully, from behind a tiny bunch of cherries.

Fiona picked some daisies as she continued searching for fairies, and Bluebell watched in fascination as

Fiona wove the stems into a daisy chain. It was just like the chain of tiny blue speedwell blossoms that she'd made to decorate her bed canopy. It looked like Fiona shared her love of making things!

Ten minutes later, the girls had checked the whole flowerbed. Katy threw herself down on the grass. "I'm all hot and sticky now. I wish this park had a pool!"

Fiona wandered over to the cherry tree and picked up something from the long grass underneath it. "Look what I've found!"

She held up a delicate dandelion seed-head. "If we make a wish on this, the fairies might hear us and make it come true."

Up in the tree, Bluebell, Rose, Ivy and Daisy peeped out from the leaves delightedly.

"Really?" Katy asked, with wide eyes. "What do we have to do?"

"I'll say the wish out loud. And then we blow hard, so that all the seeds blow away," Fiona explained. Bluebell smiled as Fiona placed her daisy-chain crown on Katy's head. "Are you ready?"

Katy nodded.

"Here we go then. I wish…"

Bluebell's heart swelled with excitement as she watched Fiona hold up the dandelion. Something very special was about to happen.

Chapter Three

"I wish … this park could be as good as new," Fiona said, her eyes tight shut.

She and Katy blew hard and a cloud of silky, feathery dandelion seeds floated upwards. Letters started to form and the silvery wish-words hung there, as delicate as embroidery in the sky.

Bluebell's wings quivered with excitement and she only just stopped herself from doing a very Daisy-like twirl in the air!

"I'm going to make your wish come true, Fiona!" she promised.

"How exciting!" said Daisy. "What a brilliant wish, Belle!"

"Oh, I do hope the Dandelion Queen lets you grant it!" said Rose.

"Let's hurry back to the oak. The wish will soon be there and you'll need to fetch your wand!" Ivy urged, pointing at the silvery wish-words, which were now floating in the direction of Starshine Meadow.

Some wishes needed collecting and taking to the Dandelion Queen, but if a wish was made directly on a dandelion seed-head it went straight to her.

The fairies flashed into the air and sped back to Starshine Meadow. As soon as they flew over the fence, they heard a faint ringing coming from the tree.

"Listen!" Daisy cried excitedly. "It's the Dandelion Queen's clock striking inside the oak – the wish must have already arrived!"

The Dandelion Queen was waiting as Bluebell flew down and landed by the tiny arch, clutching her wand. A lot of other fairies had flown into the branches to see who would arrive to claim the wish. Ivy, Daisy and Rose landed beside them, their wings glittering in the sun.

"Your Majesty,' said Bluebell. "I have come to ask permission to grant this wish."

"Bluebell!" the queen said warmly. "Can you tell me more about the wish?"

"It was made by a girl called Fiona Lake, Your Majesty. She has wished that the neglected park in Greenthorn could be as good as new," Bluebell said.

"That's a lovely wish! I'm sure you'll grant it wonderfully!" said the Dandelion Queen. "Remember, good magic helps everyone. So the wish may come true in ways you do not expect."

"I'll remember," Belle promised.

The queen smiled again. "Hold out your wand." She shook her starry dandelion wand, and a fountain of wish-dust shot towards Bluebell's wand. It glimmered with tiny, silvery dandelion seeds. "Use the magic wisely. The wish-dust's power will start to fade after the crescent moon," she explained.

"Thank you, Your Majesty."
Bluebell's tummy fizzed with
excitement as she watched the
shining blue star on her wand
twinkle with its new power.

All the watching fairies cheered
and waved. "Good luck, Belle!" they
called as Bluebell flew off across
Starshine Meadow.

Bluebell smiled – she felt both
excited and nervous. The crescent
moon was in seven days. She had
until then to grant Fiona's wish, find
the rare white bluebell, and make a
special bowl to hold the tonic!

Ivy, Rose, and Daisy caught up
with Bluebell and they all sat on the
fence, looking over towards
Greenthorn.

"Have you any ideas about granting Fiona's wish?" asked Ivy.

"Well firstly, the flowers and grass in the park look very tired and thirsty," Bluebell said thoughtfully. "I want to do something to help them, but we couldn't possibly water them all."

"Garden flowers really suffer in hot weather," Rose agreed. "They're not as strong as wild flowers."

"I know!" Daisy cried eagerly. "Why don't we wait until the Dandelion Queen has made the oak's tonic, and borrow some for the flowers in the park!"

"It's a good idea. But the Dandelion Queen is making the tonic especially for the great oak," Rose said gently. "I don't think it'd work on anything else."

"Oh yes," Daisy said thoughtfully. "It's a shame the tonic won't work on clearing away litter either!"

"Yes, that's the second bit of the wish, tidying up the park," Bluebell said. Suddenly an idea popped into her head, and she looked at the others excitedly. "You remember the mosaic that Fiona and Katy's dad helped to make?"

Rose nodded. "It's got bits missing and it's splashed with paint."

"Yes," said Bluebell. "But what if it was cleaned up and repaired? That would help give the park a makeover and show everyone that people care about it, wouldn't it?"

"That's a great idea!" Ivy and Rose chorused. "But how are you going to arrange that?"

"I think I need to get Fiona involved," Bluebell said. "I know she loves making things. First thing tomorrow, I'll fly over to her school."

Suddenly Ivy gave an excited little cry and fluttered down to some ivy that was scrambling up one of the fence posts nearby. "An eight-pointed leaf, right under my nose! What brilliant luck!"

"Well done, Ivy!" Bluebell, Daisy and Rose congratulated her. Ivy

picked the leaf and they all flew over to the oak, where a team of the queen's helpers were busy collecting and storing ingredients.

"Now I can come with you tomorrow to find Fiona, if you like, and keep an eye out for a white bluebell!" said Ivy.

"Thanks Ivy, that's brilliant!" said Bluebell, beaming. "See you all tomorrow."

An amazing sunset streaked the sky with salmon-pink clouds. It tinged Bluebell's wings with pink as she flew towards her soft bed beneath a tiny forest of ferns.

She waved back to the others. "Sweet dreams!"

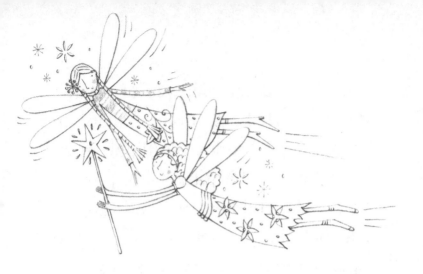

Chapter Four

The following morning, Bluebell and Ivy flew over to the park. The streets were busy with people and there were lots of children walking to school. It was already hot and the air smelt of dusty pavements and cars.

Bluebell pointed to three familiar figures. "Look! There's Fiona and Katy with their dad!"

She and Ivy followed at a safe distance. Mr Lake dropped Katy off, then waved goodbye to Fiona at a school gate a bit further on. Just before the children filed indoors, Bluebell and Ivy whizzed through an open window into Fiona's classroom.

"Where shall we hide?"asked Ivy.

Bluebell pointed to a colourful display about recycling. Food boxes and packaging were stuck on the wall near photos showing them being turned back into kitchen rolls, cards and newspapers. "How about hiding in that cereal box?"

The fairies had only just darted inside the box, when Fiona's class came in with their teacher. As soon as the register had been taken, the teacher handed everyone a large sheet of paper.

"Remember that our project for this term is recycling," the teacher said, with a smile. "Last week we made our great recycling machine. This week I'd like you to do a drawing or a painting to show how recycling can work in our daily life. You can start straight away. I'll come round to you all in turn."

There was a buzz of voices as everyone settled down.

Fiona immediately began drawing. Completely engrossed, she

frowned with concentration as she worked.

Cautiously, Ivy and Bluebell peeped out of the cereal box. Fiona was drawing a park, with brightly coloured, animal-shaped recycling bins. Children were dropping drinks cans into the bins.

"Fiona's great at art, isn't she?" said Ivy.

"Yes," Bluebell answered. "That's why she's the perfect person to help get the mosaic repaired. I just have to get her imagination working so that she'll come up with the idea herself."

Ivy watched as Bluebell used the end of her wand to poke a small hole in the back of the cereal packet.

Very quietly,
she tore tiny strips
of paper from
the display,
pulled them
into the box and
handed them to Ivy.

When there was a little pile of
paper scraps, Bluebell tapped it with
her wand and whispered,

Wishes big and wishes small,
With my wand I'll grant them all!

There was a bright golden flash
and the scraps turned into a tiny
painting that glittered and shimmered
with fairy light.

"Oh, it's so pretty," Ivy breathed.

The painting was about as big as
four postage stamps and was made
entirely from foil, sweet wrappers and
shiny plastic. It was a picture of a
tree with fairies dancing round it,
and the tiny pieces fitting together
made it look like a mosaic.

"Now we just have to make
sure Fiona sees it," Bluebell said.

She tapped the cereal box very

gently with her wand, so that it
sparkled like a fairy lantern.

Very carefully, she and Ivy
carried the painting to the open end
of the box, and tipped it out. The
painting floated to the floor and lay
there, glowing softly.

Fiona looked up just as Bluebell
and Ivy dodged out of sight.

Bluebell saw her frown as she

noticed the sparkling cereal box. She got up and came towards it, but stopped when she noticed the tiny, glittering painting on the floor.

"She's seen it!" Bluebell grasped Ivy's arm in excitement. She tapped the cereal box with her wand to stop it glowing, before anyone else noticed it.

Fiona bent down and picked up the fairy painting. Her eyes widened as she brought it back to her desk and sat looking at it as it lay in the palm of her hand. "Where did this come from?" she whispered. "It's made of tiny bits of recycled stuff, just like a mosaic. How clever!"

Fiona chewed her lip, as she seemed to think of something. She waited for Mrs Malik to make her way round the class. "Look what I've found, Mrs Malik. I don't know whose it is, but it's given me an idea."

Some of the other children wandered over, and there were gasps of delight as everyone admired the tiny painting.

"Are you sure no one in here made it?" said the teacher, looking puzzled.

"Maybe it got here by magic!" suggested one of the kids.

Everyone laughed, and Fiona smiled too. "Maybe we could design a new mosaic for the park out of recycled things. Like the one my dad made with his class."

"I know the one," said her teacher. "But I didn't realize your dad helped make it. That must have been almost twenty years ago."

"Yes, it was. And it's looking a bit scruffy now," Fiona said. "Maybe we could get permission to repair the old mosaic as part of our recycling project. And if we made a new mosaic out of recycled materials, we could put it up next to the old one…" She stopped, looking embarrassed.

"That picture's worked brilliantly," Ivy whispered, impressed.

"Yes," said Bluebell happily. "Fiona's full of ideas!"

The teacher stared at Fiona in astonishment. "That's a wonderful idea, Fiona! What does everyone else think about making this our class project?"

"It's a great idea!" someone called out.

"And maybe we could clear up the litter too?" another child said.

Mrs Malik looked as excited as the children. "Well, let's get cracking! It's breaktime now, so I'll go and make some phone calls to the council and talk to the head. I'm sure they'll love Fiona's idea."

Bluebell and Ivy hugged each other with delight as the children began going out to the playground. Fiona tucked the tiny fairy painting into her notebook. As soon as the room was empty, the fairies flew out of the classroom window, heading back towards Starshine Meadow.

"You're so clever, Belle! Fiona's wish is starting to come true and she's the one who's making it happen!" said Ivy.

Bluebell nodded, feeling happy for Fiona, but that was only part of her plan. "We still have to do something about the flowers and grass. There's such a lot of work — I'm going to need everyone's help!"

As Bluebell and Ivy were heading back towards Starshine Meadow, they spotted Rose and Daisy flying along carrying a large spider-silk bag between them.

It looked like Daisy had found the petal from a daisy with a hundred petals and Rose had found her rose from a bush with no thorns. Bluebell felt a little pang of worry. She still had to find a white bluebell, and make her bowl, but at least there were six days left until the crescent moon.

"How did you get on?" Daisy and Rose chorused.

Bluebell told them the good news about Fiona's class project and her idea for a new mosaic.

"You're doing really well with Fiona's wish," Daisy said, admiringly. "Is there anything we can do?"

"Yes!" Bluebell said. "Will you all come with me to the park tonight and bring your wands? I've got an idea about helping the flowers and grass. And Rose? I've got something special to ask you – could you write a poem, please? Something to give the plants an extra magical boost?"

Rose's tiny face lit up. "I'd love to. Leave it to me!"

Stars glittered in the dark-blue sky as Belle and her friends flew across the sleepy village. The curved slice of the moon was almost a perfect crescent.

The fairies landed on a branch in the cherry tree and looked round anxiously. Long shadows stretched across the grass and a woodpigeon's hollow cry echoed in the warm night.

"The park seems bigger than I remembered it," Ivy commented.

"There's a lot of work to do for just four fairies," Daisy said, nibbling her nail.

"Don't forget I have the wish-dust!" Bluebell said. "Hold out your wands." Rose, Daisy and Ivy did so.

Wish-dust, wish-dust, hear my spell,
Help fairy friends do their work well!

Belle shook her wand. There was a golden flash and a small shower of glowing dandelion seeds shot towards Ivy, Daisy and Rose's wands.

"Let's get to work!" cried Daisy.

Daisy and Ivy sped across the
grass, whispering and waving their
wands. As they flew to and fro, a
fountain of glowing fairy rain
whooshed out, sprinkling the grass
with crystal drops. Rose and Bluebell
flew back and forth over clumps of
flowers, singing to them. A waterfall

of glowing drops like tiny jewels poured out of their wands, and showered on to the dusty blossoms.

Dawn wasn't far away when the fairies gathered back in the cherry tree.

"The grass looks a bit fresher and the flowers seem happier," said Ivy.

"Yes, but they're still looking thirsty. Maybe Rose's poem will help," said Belle.

Rose flew to the end of a branch and took a deep breath.

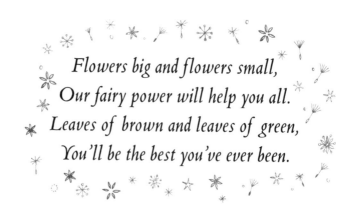

Flowers big and flowers small,
Our fairy power will help you all.
Leaves of brown and leaves of green,
You'll be the best you've ever been.

As Rose paused, the leaves and grass stood up and turned a deeper green.

In bright sunshine and without rain,
We have made you flourish again.
In this pretty park you'll grow,
And Fiona's heart will be aglow.

Once again, Rose paused. The flowers gave a little shake and lifted their heads, glowing with fresh colour.

The work that we have just begun,
Will bring delight to everyone.
For one girl's wish and loving care,
Will make a park for all to share.

As Rose finished her poem, Bluebell flew over and gave her a hug. "That was a wonderful poem. And it's worked really well! I think it's time for us to go. Thank you all so much. I could never have done this by myself!"

Bluebell led the way as they all flew back to Starshine Meadow. She had barely crawled into her moss-lined bed, with its fringe of blue speedwell blossoms, before she fell fast asleep.

Chapter Five

Over the next five days, fairies flew busily back and forth across Starshine Meadow bringing ingredients for the oak's tonic.

Bluebell had been back over to the park to search for a white bluebell. She still hadn't found one, but a poster pinned to a noticeboard had caught her eye.

PARK MAKE OVER DAY

Come and help us This Saturday

ALL WELCOME !

Bluebell had smiled to herself, delighted. Fiona's wish was coming true! All Bluebell had to do was finish her bowl and find the white bluebell and then she'd have plenty of time to spend at the park on Makeover Day.

But things hadn't quite gone to plan. It was Saturday, and Bluebell was sitting on her bed, weaving

silvery grasses into her bowl. She was
running out of time to get everything
finished. She'd searched everywhere
for a white bluebell but she still
hadn't found one, and the bowl
wasn't quite finished either.

As Bluebell added some pretty,
starry moss, Daisy appeared and sat
cross-legged on a nearby clover leaf.

"What do you think?" Bluebell
asked, showing her the bowl.

"It's quite pretty…"
Daisy said tactfully.

"But it's missing
something?"
Bluebell put her
head on one side.
"Maybe it needs
something sparkly."

Bluebell had a sudden thought, and leaped into the air. "And I know just where to look! The park!"

"And that gives you the perfect excuse to see what's happening at the Makeover Day!" said Daisy grinning. "I'll come too!"

As they zoomed across Greenthorn, they heard voices and laughter. The park was full of adults and children, hard at work. Bluebell

and Daisy hovered high in the air to
watch what was going on.

"Gosh! I didn't think this many
people would turn up!" said Bluebell.

Children were collecting litter,
supervised by Mrs Malik. Mr Lake
and a stocky man with fair hair were
cleaning paint off the old mosaic. Val
Roberts, with Muppet at her heels,
was next to them, scrubbing the tiles
until they gleamed.

"I bet that's Val's son, Andrew, with Mr Lake," Bluebell said. "He's the one who thought he saw a fairy as a boy. I wish we could show him he was right!"

"And look, there's Fiona and Katy," said Daisy.

Bluebell spotted the girls, talking to a woman wearing a T-shirt with *The Greenthorn Herald* on it. "Let's go and listen to what they're saying," she said, flying down to hide behind a litter-bin. Daisy quickly followed her.

"This is a drawing of the new mosaic, which my class is making at school from recycled rubbish. It's going to go there, next to the one my dad's class made," Fiona told the reporter.

"I'm surprised to see so many people in this park, especially children," the reporter said. "What gave your class the idea to come here and do a big clear-up?"

"We're doing a project on recycling," Fiona explained, "and I had an idea to make Dad's old mosaic look as good as new. Then the idea just grew into a park makeover day."

"And have you seen how wonderful the grass and plants look?" said Val, appearing at Fiona's side. "Someone's been hard at work here. Doesn't all this show how much we care about this park? We need to keep it for our children and grandchildren to enjoy…"

Bluebell and Ivy exchanged gleeful glances. All their hard work had been noticed.

Suddenly Daisy tugged at Bluebell's hand. "Oh look! Over there in that flowerbed. Do you see what I see?"

Bluebell looked down and spotted something beside some yellow pansies. It was a silvery white bluebell! Her heart lifted with joy as she flew over and picked one tiny stem.

"Thank you very much," she whispered to the plant. "This is going to help the great oak."

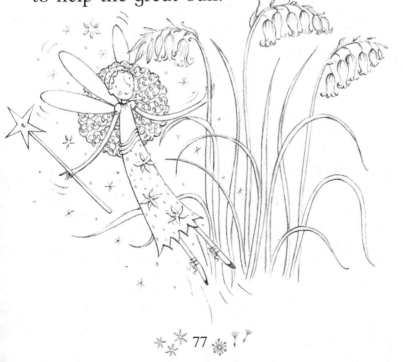

Rose and Ivy fluttered down under the ferns, into the shade of Bluebell's bed canopy. All the ingredients had been gathered, and soon the crescent moon would rise and the Dandelion Queen would make the tonic.

"I've just taken the final ingredient to the queen's helpers. The white bluebell!" Bluebell told them.

"Well done!" said Rose. "It was a hard thing to find."

"Daisy spotted it, luckily for me!" Bluebell said. "But I still haven't quite finished my bowl!" Her wings fluttered in panic.

"Don't worry. We'll help you," said Ivy.

"Just show us what to do," said
Rose.

"Oh, thank you!" Belle beamed
gratefully at her friends.

All the fairies leaned back against
Bluebell's cool moss pillows as she
showed them how to make little
blue, silver and gold flowers out of
her store of sweet wrappers.

As they worked, Bluebell told Rose and Ivy about the park.

"And you should have seen how hard Fiona's class were working. The park looks great!" Daisy added.

"So Fiona's wish is coming true in the most wonderful way!" said Rose.

"Yes," said Ivy, hugging Bluebell. "The Dandelion Queen said that good magic works for everyone, didn't she? Lots of people are going to enjoy the park!"

"There!" Bluebell said at last. "It's finished. And just in time! We'd better take it over to the oak tree."

Bluebell, Rose, Ivy and Daisy threaded their way through the ferns, holding the bowl between them.

Everything was ready. The soft light of the crescent moon filtered down through the branches, silvering the wings of the fairies gathered there. They were sorting ingredients into piles, with the help of the Dandelion Queen. She wore a magnificent silver and pearl-white gown. Her crown was a starburst of shimmering, feathery dandelion seeds.

"What a beautiful bowl," she said, as Bluebell and her friends drifted down and placed it at her feet. "It's perfect. Thank you."

"We all made it together," said Bluebell.

The queen smiled at Ivy, Rose and Daisy. "My thanks to you too," she said. "How are you getting on with Fiona's wish, Belle?"

"Very well, Your Majesty." Bluebell told the queen all about helping the flowers and grass in the park and about Fiona's class project.

The queen smiled again. "Well done, Belle. It sounds as if you helped make Fiona very happy. Don't forget the wish-dust will start to lose its power after tonight."

"I won't, Your Majesty,"
Bluebell said, feeling very proud. She
had one last thing to do tomorrow,
and Ivy, Rose and Daisy were going
to help her.

All the fairies gathered close. The
queen waved her hand and the fairy
helpers began putting ingredients into
Bluebell's bowl. They dissolved into a
golden liquid as the queen stirred the
mixture with her wand. When the
final ingredient had been added, the
queen spread her arms wide.

Fairies all have brought to you,
Flowers and leaves for the magic dew!
Golden rain and silver snow,
Power of sun — make leaves grow!

She shook her wand. There was a bright flash and a shower of tiny golden dandelion petals floated into the bowl.

Bluebell lined up excitedly with Ivy, Daisy and Rose as the queen shook her wand again. A single drop of glowing tonic was transferred to each fairy's wand. When all the fairies had their drops, they fluttered up high above the oak in a sparkling golden cloud against the night sky.

All together they shook their wands and let the drops fall. A soft

golden mist that smelled of honey
and the freshest rain drifted down
over the oak, and almost at once tiny
green shoots appeared on the ends of
the branches.

"Look! The oak's growing new leaves!" Rose said happily.

All the fairies joined hands and danced around the tree, singing joyfully.

Chapter Six

The next morning, Bluebell flew
over to the little park with Ivy, Daisy
and Rose. She couldn't wait to see
how the park looked after the
Makeover Day.

The park was full of children,
playing games, having picnics with
their parents, and playing on the
swings and slide.

"Wow!" said Daisy. "Look at all these people!"

Bluebell spotted Fiona and Katy at once. They were standing looking at the old mosaic. The splashes of paint had gone, the missing tiles had been replaced, and the mosaic gleamed with new life.

Even better, the new mosaic had

EVERYONE WELCOME !

GREENTHORN

PARK

been made next to the old one. Belle
gasped with delight. It was a tree
with spreading branches against a
bright blue sky, and dancing around
the trunk was a circle of fairies – the
same as in the fairy painting she had
given Fiona!

"It's beautiful," said Rose. Daisy
and Ivy nodded.

Bluebell flew closer, drifting down on top of the playground wall. The other fairies followed her.

"The fairies look so real," Katy said, tracing one with her finger. "How did you draw them like that?"

"I don't know," Fiona said. "I just seemed to see the pictures in my head – like magic."

"Hey! Girls! I've got something to show you!" Their dad came over, waving a newspaper. "Look at this! It says here that the council has changed its mind about making the park into a car park. It's going to spend more money doing it up." He looked at them and grinned. "And guess what – it's putting in a paddling pool!"

"That's fantastic!" Fiona cried, grabbing Katy and twirling her round.

"There's Val and Muppet! I'll go and tell them the good news," said their dad.

"Can we go on another fairy hunt?" Katy whispered to Fiona.

"In a bit, but first I just want to enjoy the park," Fiona said. "Why don't you go over and say hello to Muppet?"

Fiona headed over to the shade of the cherry tree and sat down on the cool grass. "Everything's perfect," she breathed, as she watched everyone having fun.

"Not quite!" Bluebell whispered, bubbling with happiness. Her task was almost done, but she had one final thing to do – she had to leave a fairy charm for Fiona.

All the fairies fluttered down into a bush beside Fiona. Bluebell spotted a pink sweet wrapper tucked right into the bottom of the bush. It was perfect. Together they whispered,

Fairies all will make a charm,
To bring good luck and do no harm.

Bluebell waved her wand. There was a gold flash and a final shower of sparkly wish-dust shot out and covered the pink wrapper. All the fairies blew gently and tiny writing appeared in glittery gold letters.

Gold of sun and sky of blue
This fairy promise is for you
We dwell where silver streams do flow
Flowers bloom and grasses grow
Whenever needed, we hear the call
And bring good luck to one and all

Holding the wrapper between them, the fairies flew out and dropped it just above Fiona. They had only just hidden themselves again, when she opened her eyes.

"Oh, what's this?" Fiona gasped as the twinkling wrapper drifted down. Her face lit up with wonder as she stared at it, and she read the poem aloud, running her fingers over the glittering lettering.

The second she had finished, the wrapper whooshed out of her hand and disappeared in a cloud of sparkly golden dust.

"Maybe there really are fairies in the park," Fiona whispered, her eyes shining. "And wishes really can come true!"